Dear Parent:

It is my pleasure to present my book "Where's The Green Pea?"

I wrote the story and the accompanying music and lyrics for our grandaughter when she was four years old and being seventy, myself, I tried to imbue the simple story with "old fashioned" values of family relationships, heeding instructions and cooperating with others ... especially those you love. I then added a sprinkling of lighthearted thoughts and music.

Thank you for your interest.

Grandpa Mike-e-e

Grandpa Mike-e-e

~ ~ ~

I am indebted to librarians Anita LaSpina and Maureen Chiofaro, for their continuous advice and encouragement; to teachers Sue Carey and Georgette Brown for reading my copy and paying attention to my expressed concerns; to Leslie Herrmann, Director of The Learnabout Nursery School,whose staff taught "Where's The Green Pea?" to the students and needled me to "Go!" and to Emanuel Focarazzo, a young, musical brain surgeon, who has the capability to look into my head and locate the notes I described floating around there. He also permits me to share his youth.

Without my wife of forty-seven years, my sweetheart, no way would this book ever have seen the light of day. Her constant tugging and constructive criticism made it possible. She's also the grandma singing "Where's The Green Pea?" and reading the story on the audio cassette.

Wow-e-e!

Where's the Green Pea?

Story by
MICHAEL GREENE

Illustrated by
RAYMOND F. RINGSTON JR.

TUESDAY'S CHILD PUBLISHING
Somers, New York

Michael Greene:

Michael Greene has planned more than 40,000 children's rooms and is a designer/consultant for children's furniture manufacturers. He has lectured on children's rooms to women's organizations and is an international columnist for the Cahners Business Newspapers — Furniture/Today and Home Textiles Today.

~   ~   ~

A special thanks to Carla Orlando for
lending her special voice to Grandpa Mike-e-e's
songs: "Jenni's Prayer" and "Dancing."

"WHERE'S THE GREEN PEA?" Copyright © 1991 by Michael Greene.
All rights reserved. Printed in the United States of America.
For Information: Tuesday's Child Publishing Ltd.
           619B Heritage Hills
           Somers, New York 10589

Library of Congress Catalog Card Number:
Greene, Michael
91-91536

ISBN 1-881134-00-8

"Where's the Green Pea?"
Design & Illustrations by Raymond Ringston
Summary: While Jamie is helping her mother make vegetable soup she
discovers that the little green pea is missing and the other vegetables
team up and volunteer to help her find him.

1. Vegetable-Fiction. 2. Colors

First Printing, 1992
Second Printing, 1998

10 9 8 5 4 3 2 1

Many an afternoon Jamie and her mother worked together in the kitchen. Jamie would mix the batter for all kinds of delicious muffins and once she even mixed the batter for her cousin Josh's big, birthday cake.

Because Jamie was careful she was allowed to decorate the muffins with chocolate, strawberry or vanilla icing and top them off with sprinkles and raisins or fresh strawberries. She especially loved to put the icing on, because some of it would always stick to her fingers and she would quickly lick it off before it had a chance to set.

All by herself, Jamie learned how to make squiggly patterns with the icing so that every muffin had an inviting look.

"Remember, Jamie" her mother taught, "don't jump up to hurry and do things. Always think ahead and follow instructions because, here in the kitchen, some things are hot and can burn you if you're not careful."

Jamie's mother was real proud of her because Jamie did listen and was very cooperative. When her work was done, she always helped her mother clean the kitchen counter, sweep the floor and put the baking utensils back in the drawer to use another day.

Jamie and her mother grew to be a great team.

One day, Jamie was in the kitchen helping her mother prepare a healthy vegetable soup in a large, deep kettle filled with water.

She had tomatoes so red, lettuce so green, and carrots so, orange but she couldn't find the little green pea.

"Green pea! Green pea!" she called. "Are you hiding from me?" There was no answer.

Jamie then asked the onion so white, the string bean so green, and the squash so yellow, if they had seen the little green pea.

They all shook their heads, sadly.

She then turned and asked the pepper so red, who answered: "I saw him a short while ago, but he just went and disappeared.

"My oh! my," whispered everyone.

"Oh!" cried Jamie. "The little green pea must be lost. I've got to find him before he gets hurt. Who will help me search for him? Because if we work together, like a team, then I know good things will happen.

What do you all say?"

And—**WOW-e-e!**—all the vegetables raised their hands in unison, and yelled: "Yes! Yes! We'll do our best." And Jamie was delighted to hear such a willingness to cooperate. She then asked her mother if she could borrow the large flashlight; the one the family kept in the top drawer of the kitchen cabinet to use in an emergency, when the electric power would sometimes go off during a storm.

"Is everyone ready?" questioned Jamie, as she clicked the flashlight on.

"We sure are!" came the answer.

8

And there, to Jamie's amazement, stood her team friends all dressed up for the search: The tomato so red had put on his fresh, white sneakers with red shoelaces. The lettuce so green was carrying her parasol umbrella. The carrot so orange was wearing his best striped tie, while the pepper so red was showing off her classy wide·brimmed hat with ribbon and bow. And standing taller than all the others,was the squash so yellow wearing a nifty cap and resting his squash racket on his shoulder.

Out in front, ready to lead the search, stood the onion so white, holding a shiny baton, and the string bean so green, with her bass fiddle on wheels, all set to play the "Where's The Green Pea?" song. What a colorful sight it was!

"Why are you all dressed up?" asked Jamie with surprise.

"Because vegetables and fine dressing always go, naturally, together," answered the onion so white, proudly. "If we're trying to do our best,then we've got to look our best." He then raised his shiny baton and called out:

"Everybody march!"

11

And off the team went, zig zagging around and around the kitchen table legs, marching up, over and down the kitchen chairs, making sure to check all the dark corners. And as they marched, each one sang: "Green pea! Green pea! are you hiding from me?" while Jamie directed her flashlight beam across the kitchen floor as she thought to herself: "My goodness! The team looks just like a marching rainbow!"

Suddenly, the carrot so orange started to jump up and down, causing his striped tie to go flapping all over his face, and shouted: "Here he is! Here he is!" And sure enough, there was the little green pea hidden away in a dark corner, looking very, very sad and lonely.

Everyone cheered as Jamie ran over to pick him up.

"Be careful, Jamie," warned the onion so white. "He's so little and soft you'll squash him."

"Thank you, onion so white," answered Jamie. "That's thoughtful thinking and real teamwork."

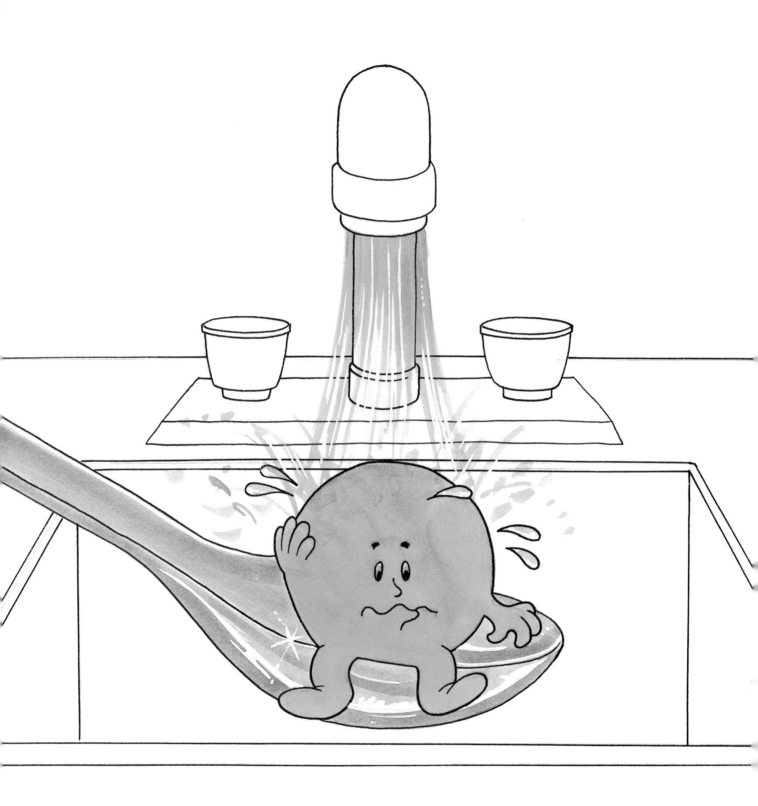

Quickly, she found a large soup spoon onto which she carefully placed the little green pea—who was awfully dusty. Then, with even more care, she carried him to the kitchen sink and gave him a cool, gentle shower under the faucet, and tenderly rolled him dry on a paper towel, to keep him from catching cold. The little green pea finally smiled. He was safe and among friends.

He was very, very happy.

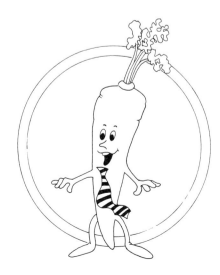

"Green pea, green pea, why were you hiding from me?" asked Jamie, softly, as she held him in the palm of her hand.

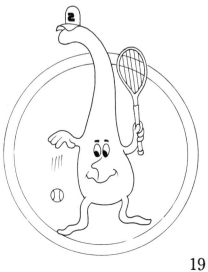

"I wasn't hiding from you, Jamie," explained the little green pea. "While I was on the kitchen counter with all the big vegetables, waiting my turn to jump into the deep kettle filled with water, I wanted to tell you something important. So I raised my hand, politely, but you didn't pay attention. So I then raised both my hands and before you could notice me —Whoops!— being so round—I rolled right off the kitchen counter and across the kitchen floor."

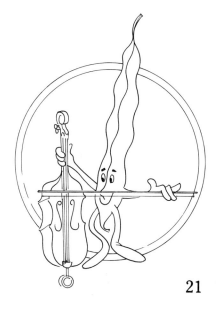

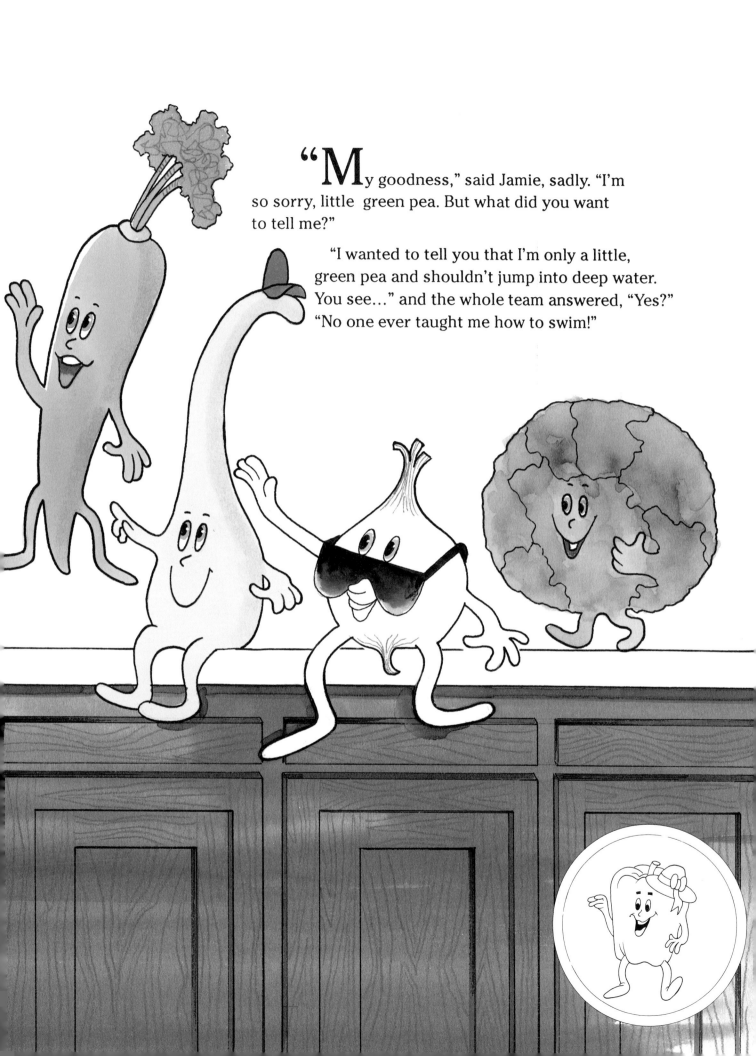

"My goodness," said Jamie, sadly. "I'm so sorry, little green pea. But what did you want to tell me?"

"I wanted to tell you that I'm only a little, green pea and shouldn't jump into deep water. You see..." and the whole team answered, "Yes?" "No one ever taught me how to swim!"

W e-l-l!

When the team heard that, they all gathered around the little green pea and cheered: Green pea! Green pea! You're surely our best buddy!"

At which point, the tall squash lifted the little green pea high above everyone's head and told him in a booming voice: "Green pea! no matter how little you are you will always look ten foot tall to us. Because now we know that you always think before you jump."

Everyone applauded and the whole team ran around and hugged one another. What a happy moment!

B ut the happiest moment was Jamie's … who thought to herself: "My mommy once told me the same thing: Always think before you jump!"

WHERE'S THE GREEN PEA?

Vegetable Plate Menu

A - What page is he on?
B - What is his name?
C - What color should he be?
D - What is he wearing?
E - What is he holding?

A - What page is he on?
B - What is his name?
C - What color should he be?
D - What is he wearing?

A - What page is she on?
B - What is her name?
C - What color should she be?
D - What is she wearing?

A - What page is he on?
B - What is his name?
C - What color should he be?
D - What is he wearing?

A - What page is she on?
B - What is her name?
C - What color should she be?
D - What is she carrying?

A - What page is he on?
B - What is his name?
C - What color should he be?
D - What is he holding?

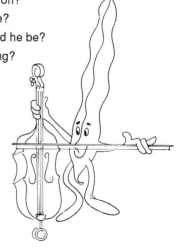

A - What page is he on?
B - What is his name?
C - What color should he be?
D - What is he wearing?
E - What is he holding?

WHERE'S THE GREEN PEA?

Words and Music by Michael Greene © 1989
Arrangement by Emanuel Focarazzo.

2. We were making hot soup, my mommy and me, when you rolled off the
table to a place I can't see. Green pea. Green pea. I Search for you
endlessly. Green pea. Green pea. We're all so very hungry.

3. I've got onions so white, and string beans so green, squash that is
yellow, but where's my Green pea? Green pea. Green pea. Oh, where - oh,
where can you be? Green pea. Green pea. We'll have no soup without thee.

4. I've got peppers so red, and some that are green,
a few that are yellow, but where's my Green pea? Green pea.
Roll out to where I can see. Take care, take care. I'm still your best buddy.